The Little Rabbit

A Random House PICTUREBACK®

The Little Rabbit

Story by **Judy Dunn**
Photographs by **Phoebe Dunn**

Random House 🏠 New York

Text copyright © 1980 by Judy Dunn Spangenberg. Photographs copyright © 1980 by Phoebe Dunn. All rights reserved under International and Pan-American Copyright Conventions. Published in the United States by Random House, Inc., New York, and simultaneously in Canada by Random House of Canada Limited, Toronto.

Library of Congress Cataloging in Publication Data: Dunn, Judy. The little rabbit. SUMMARY: Sarah's Easter gift rabbit becomes her constant companion and eventually gives birth to seven little bunnies. [1. Rabbits–Fiction] I. Dunn, Phoebe. II. Title PZ7.D92158Li [E] 79-5241 ISBN: 0-394-84377-0 (trade), ISBN: 0-394-94377-5 (lib. bdg.) Manufactured in the United States of America 1 2 3 4 5 6 7 8 9 0

One Easter, Sarah
found a little rabbit
in her Easter basket.
She was nestled beside
two eggs.

The little rabbit was soft and white. She had bright
pink eyes, long ears that were pink inside, and a tiny
pink nose that was always wiggling. Sarah loved her new
friend very much.

Sarah let the little rabbit play in the grass while she tried to think of just the right name for her. There were some tiny yellow flowers nearby called buttercups. "That's a nice name!" said Sarah to her little friend. "I'll call *you* Buttercup, too."

Sarah took good care of Buttercup. Every day she visited the new red hutch, bringing food pellets and fresh water. Then she watched Buttercup eat and drink.

Sarah's other friends loved Buttercup, too. After school they hurried over to Sarah's house and played with the little rabbit. Buttercup was always happy to be the center of attention. All the children wished they had a rabbit of their own.

One afternoon Sarah took
Buttercup out to the meadow and
fell asleep. But Buttercup did
not want to sleep. She was soon
hopping off to meet new friends.
First she came upon a slow-moving
turtle, and then she met a
beautiful orange and black
butterfly. There was so much to
see and do out in the world.

But what was that!
Buttercup was startled
by something moving
in the ferns. It was
another rabbit.

The other rabbit was a wild rabbit. He was quite different
from Buttercup. He had large brown eyes and brown fur that
helped him to hide from his enemies. The two rabbits watched
each other for a long time. Then they hopped away.

Buttercup was hungry,
so she nibbled some grass
beside a rhubarb patch.
Suddenly it began to rain.
She ran for cover and got
stuck between some stalks.
Then she sat and watched
the rain. She felt very
small and very lonely.

When Sarah woke up, she searched all over for Buttercup and finally found her.

Sarah and Buttercup went everywhere together. Sometimes they went on picnics in the woods. Sarah always brought along a carrot for Buttercup.

Sarah was very proud of her rabbit. Over the next few months Buttercup grew bigger and bigger. Soon she was ready to have babies of her own. Sarah put a nesting box filled with clean straw into the hutch.

Buttercup pulled fur from her coat to make a soft, warm nest for her babies. Then she waited. Sarah visited the hutch often, but nothing happened.

Then one morning
Sarah looked into the
hutch and saw seven
baby rabbits in the nest.

"Oh, Buttercup," she
said, "you're a mother!"
Sarah was so happy to
see the babies.

The babies grew fast. Soon they were big enough to climb out of the nesting box and look around. They were lively and curious, and as soft and white as their mother. Now Sarah had to think of names for all of them!

Since there were seven
baby rabbits, Sarah decided
to name them after the
seven days of the week—
Sunday, Monday, Tuesday,
Wednesday, Thursday,
Friday, and Saturday.

Soon the little rabbits were big enough to go outside. Sunday, Monday, and Tuesday stayed in Sarah's lap, but the others jumped out. Wednesday sat under the daffodils, Thursday sniffed violets, and Friday hopped through the grass.

Little Saturday went farther
than any of her brothers and
sisters. Soon she found herself
in a sea of tiny blue flowers.
There were flowers everywhere.
Saturday stopped right where
she was because she didn't know
what else to do. She was lost,
but Sarah soon found her.

It was time for the rabbits to go home. Sarah couldn't get them all back by herself, so she called for her father. Together they collected the little rabbits and put them back into the hutch with Buttercup.

"Sarah," said her father, "there are just too many rabbits, and they're getting bigger every day. It's time you found good homes for Buttercup's babies." Sarah wanted to keep them all, but she knew her father was right. There *were* too many rabbits, and the hutch was crowded.

So the next day Sarah offered one or two of Buttercup's babies to each of her friends. Monday went home with Kate, and Billy chose Tuesday for his pet.

Wednesday and Thursday rode home in Jeff's bicycle basket. By the end of the day, all of Buttercup's babies had new homes, and Sarah's friends were proud to have rabbits of their own.

Sarah and Buttercup were happy to be alone together, just as they were in the beginning.

"I love you, Buttercup," said Sarah as she stroked her rabbit's soft white fur. But Buttercup just wiggled her pink nose.